The Canning Season

The Canning Season

by **Margaret Carlson**

with illustrations by **Kimanne Smith**

a first person book

Carolrhoda Books, Inc./Minneapolis

This story first appeared in the September 1995 issue of *Cricket,* vol. 23, no. 1.

Carolrhoda Books, Inc., c/o The Lerner Publishing Group
241 First Avenue North, Minneapolis, MN 55401 U.S.A.

Website address: www.lernerbooks.com

LIBRARY OF CONGRESS CATALOGING-IN-PUBLICATION DATA

Carlson, Margaret.
   The canning season / by Margaret Carlson ; illustrated by Kimanne Smith.
     p. cm. — (A first person book)
   Summary: When her friendship with Peggy begins to unravel because of racial prejudice, Peggie's sadness eases as she basks in the warmth of family love one day during the canning season.
   ISBN 1-57505-260-1
   I. Afro-Americans—Juvenile fiction. [1. Afro-Americans—Fiction. 2. Prejudices—Fiction. 3. Friendship—Fiction.] I. Smith, Kimanne, ill. II. Title. III. Series.
PZ7.C2166335Can 1999
[E]—dc21   98-14061

Manufactured in the United States of America
1 2 3 4 5 6 – JR – 04 03 02 01 00 99

To Mom, Auntie, Grandmother,
Jennifer, Debbie, Lucille,
and my daughter, Jenna — M.C.

Especially for Kortney, Kamika, and family,
Alyson and her family, and for my daughters,
Caroline and Kristen — K.S.

Three fat fannies swayed to the gospel music
playing in the background. The music was
turned up just enough to be heard over the
five fans, carefully placed to remove the
hot, sticky air from the kitchen. It was
late August. It was 1959. The
canning season was in full swing.

Grandmother, Auntie, and Mom seemed not to notice the heat. A rhythmic *snap, snap, crack, ping* kept pace with the music as they snapped the ends off beans, broke them into halves, and tossed them into the black-and-white speckled pan.

The sounds were good. The fans hummed, the music played, and the beans clinked as they landed on the enameled surface.

Mostly, I liked to hear the occasional laughter as it rose from Grandmother, Auntie, and Mom at the sink. I strained my neck, careful not to be seen, and listened quietly in hopes of discovering the nature of their laughter. I longed for the day when I would stand beside them and share their secrets.

It was a busy time around our house during the canning season. The activity and commotion rivaled Christmas. Mom hustled about our kitchen, shouting orders and making snap decisions. "No, no, no. Don't throw that out. That isn't garbage. We'll use those cores to make apple butter." "Hey, you! Get your fingers out of there!" Or more calmly, "Add two more teaspoons of salt. Then it will be perfect."

Mom was very picky. Babies, and those who could not take orders, were kept at bay.

"Mother?" My mom was speaking to her mom. "I don't like the look of that jar of beans."

Grandmother looked at the suspect jar. "It seems just fine to me, Mary Jane. What don't you like?" Grandmother asked.

"There's a space. See, right here." Mom held the culprit up to the light. There was a thin line between the beans and the bottom of the jar. "As the beans absorb the liquid, this space will grow. I don't like it." She looked at the jar with disgust.

Grandmother and Auntie exchanged knowing glances. Mary Jane was hard to please. "It won't affect the taste, dear."

"Yes, but this jar will have to go to the back of the shelf. It doesn't look good enough for the front row," Mother decided.

The ugly jar was set aside. It seemed that segregation affected beans as well as people.

I felt like that jar of beans once. My friend, Peggy, and I were walking home from school. We decided to stop at Don's Polka Dot Dairy and spend the change burning holes in our pockets. I bought a pack of Bazooka Joe bubblegum and crammed my mouth with it. I was having difficulty breaking it down.

"I can't spend Friday night at your house," said Peggy.

I couldn't speak, so I just looked at her. She said again, "My mom said I can't stay overnight at your house anymore."

"Why not?" I was barely able to ask. It sounded more like "Wanaw?"

Peggy was my best and only friend. I was not this important to her. She was very popular. I was not. And she was very careful not to call me "best friend," as I had heard her call several other of our classmates.

We lived near each other. We were both christened Margaret and quickly nicknamed Peggy, but I spelled my name *Peggie.* We both hated Barbie dolls and loved to climb trees. We suited one another. I was satisfied.

"Mom says I can't stay at your house 'cause you've got brothers," Peggy told me.

This wasn't making any sense. We had been staying at each other's houses for years. My brothers had always been at home. Mrs. Nolan knew this. My brothers and Peggy's brothers played on all the teams together. My father and her father coached all these teams. What was she talking about?

I stared at her and began working aggressively on my gum. Was Mrs. Nolan going crazy, or what?

"You know," Peggy said, pulling on her long, straight hair. She only pulled when she was nervous. "You know," she said again, looking at me with a stupid grin on her face.

I was getting mad. "I DON'T know. What are you talking about?"

"Well, you don't have to yell at me," she said.

"Peggy," I said as if speaking to a three-year-old, "please tell me why your mother has suddenly become aware of the fact that I have several brothers."

"She knows that you have brothers," Peggy answered. "It's just that...you know...you're Negroes."

I spat out my gum, just missing her ear. She jumped but said nothing. "I see," I said out loud.

My brothers, attracted to Peggy? This was what Mrs. Nolan was afraid of.

Peggy looked like all the girls in *Seventeen* magazine. She had long, straight blond hair. She stood in front of me, her face turned down. She made designs in the dirt with the toe of her Keds, too scared to meet my eyes. That was a first.

"My mom said that you can stay at our house," she said, still not looking at me. "Why don't you ask your parents if you can spend the night with me?"

My eyes filled with tears. I tried not to see or hear her. I didn't look like Peggy Nolan, or like any of the girls in *Seventeen* magazine. But my brothers said I was pretty.

Mrs. Nolan was dead wrong. My brothers wouldn't bother her little girl.

No force of gravity could make the tears fall from my eyes. "I can't stay at your house," I said. I wanted to hurt her like she had just hurt me. I knew that this would be my last chance. I couldn't be her friend, even though I had no other friend. Not after what she had said about my family.

"Why can't you?" she asked, surprised.

"My mom said that I can't stay at your house," I replied. "Because YOU have brothers." I turned and ran home.

That was the day I got my first cup of coffee.
I grew up with the aroma of coffee in the
kitchen, fresh ground and brewed. Father said
that women engaged in endless barrages of
meaningless bibble-babble when fueled by too
much black coffee. Mother said that he was
simply jealous. I didn't care. I just wanted to
taste what smelled so good.

"What is it, dear?" Mother asked while
directing me toward an empty seat at the
kitchen table. When I didn't answer, she went
on. "Has Frank been teasing you?" I shook
my head no.

"Has Bobby been teasing you, then?"
Auntie asked. Again, no.

Mom seemed worried. "Any problems at school today?" Before I could answer, she asked, "Where's Peggy? I thought she was spending the night. Have you two been fighting?" Again, I said nothing.

Peggy and I had had our differences over the years, but Mom knew that we had never allowed these differences to prevent our sleep-overs.

"What did she say to you, Peggie?" Mom asked, sensing the intensity of my pain.

"She will never stay overnight here again," I said with a finality that surprised even me.

"Why not?" Grandmother spoke for the first time.

"Because I have Negro brothers," I answered. "Because the Nolans are afraid of them. Because I don't like Peggy and I'll never stay at her house."

No more words were spoken on the subject that day. But the generations of eyes in that room revealed the pain and sorrow of understanding.

Grandmother got up and went to the corner cupboard. She took out a tiny cup and saucer, trimmed in gold. These dishes were reserved for special occasions only. She poured a spot of hot, black brew into the cup. Everyone watched as she went to the refrigerator and took out the cream. She poured again. She then placed the cup and saucer in front of me.

I scrunched down low. I wanted to be level with the drink so I could smell as I sipped. I made a lot of noise. I took my time. I wanted to make it last forever. The warm, tawny-colored drink I had desired for so long did not disappoint me . . . like Peggy had.

My mother, my aunt, and my grandmother watched. They made no comment about my poor table manners.

After a while, the women stretched, sighed, and shuffled back to the sink to resume stuffing green beans into Mason jars. From the back, they looked like two pears and a potato. It was clear that I would never have a Barbie doll's hourglass figure.

I got up and stood next to Mom. She smiled and handed a dishtowel and jar to me. I wiped the jar clean, as I had watched her do so often, and carefully set the beans into the wire basket at my feet. Grandmother and Auntie pretended not to be watching, but I saw their smiles of approval.

"Land sakes, it's hot in here," Auntie said. She turned on the three fans Grandmother had turned off during the coffee break.

"Don't forget the music, Sis," Mom said, handing me another jar.

"Lordy, yes!" Grandmother sang, sashaying a little and brushing back a wisp of fallen white hair. "Turn up the music!"

Author's Note

Peggie's story is my story—the story of my growing up in a suburb of Minneapolis, Minnesota, in 1959. In 1959, racial prejudice was expressed differently. People did not talk openly of their feelings about racial and ethnic differences. Those who lived in the northern part of the United States often denied that racism existed where they lived. They were wrong. Even though racism was often more subtle in the North, as it is in Peggie's story, racism still existed.

In the South, Jim Crow laws were common. Many white Southerners claimed that these laws made opportunities for white people and black people separate and equal. According to these laws, white people and black people went to separate schools, sat in separate parts of buses, and were even buried in separate cemeteries. But they were not equal.

Segregated black schools were poorly supplied. Segregated white schools fared much better. Often blacks could not do basic things, such as swim in a public pool, drink from a public water fountain, sit in the front seats of a public bus, or eat at a public lunch counter.

All of these things were true in the South in 1959, when Peggie's story takes place.

In the years since, many things have changed. Jim Crow laws no longer exist. More people in the North and the South understand the destructive power of racism. However, our country is not free from racism, and the effect of racial prejudice is the same as it was in 1959. Racism still hurts. It still forces the young to grow up too fast. And it still can end a friendship, as it did for Peggie. Sadly, her story is not unique. But with love and family support, she was able to put the pain of Peggy's rejection behind her.

Since this story took place, Peggie has made many new friends of different ethnic backgrounds. Keeping a journal—and writing about this and other episodes—has helped me, the grown-up Peggie, recapture my emotions and better understand a difficult and special time in my life—the canning season of 1959.

Note to Teachers and Parents

Margaret Carlson's The Canning Season *includes many topics for further discussion. To deepen their understanding of the story, ask young readers to consider and discuss the questions below:*

1. What does Peggie, the narrator, mean when she says "It seemed like segregation affected beans as well as people"? What was segregation like? How did it make people feel? Have you ever been segregated from others?

2. Why was Mrs. Nolan afraid that one of Peggie's brothers might like Peggy Nolan? The marriage of two people from different racial backgrounds was once against the law in many states. What were the people in those states and Peggy Nolan's mom afraid of?

3. After their conversation at Don's Polka Dot Dairy, Peggie realizes she can never be Peggy Nolan's friend again. Have your friends ever disappointed you the way Peggy Nolan disappoints Peggie? How did it make you feel? How did you react? Peggie uses a simile, or a comparison using the word *like,* to describe her feelings. She says, "I felt like that jar of beans once."

In your own journal, can you use a simile to describe how you felt at an important time in your life? How do you feel about that time now? Based on your reading of this story, how do you think the narrator, Peggie, feels by the end of the day, as she sips her first cup of coffee?